For my daughters —M.W.L.

For Zachary —A.H.

THIS IS A BORZOI BOOK PUBLISHED BY ALFRED A. KNOPF

Text copyright © 2017 by Megan Wagner Lloyd

Jacket art and interior illustrations copyright © 2017 by Abigail Halpin

All rights reserved. Published in the United States by Alfred A. Knopf, an imprint of Random House Children's Books, a division of Penguin Random House LLC, New York.

Knopf, Borzoi Books, and the colophon are registered trademarks of Penguin Random House LLC.

Visit us on the Web! randomhousekids.com

Educators and librarians, for a variety of teaching tools, visit us at RHTeachersLibrarians.com

Library of Congress Cataloging-in-Publication Data
Names: Lloyd, Megan Wagner, author. | Halpin, Abigail, illustrator.
Title: Fort-building time / Megan Wagner Lloyd ; illustrated by Abigail Halpin.
Description: First edition. | New York : Alfred A. Knopf, 2017. | Summary: "An exploration of building forts throughout all four seasons." —Provided by publisher | Description based on print version record and CIP data provided by publisher; resource not viewed.
Identifiers: LCCN 2016025703 (print) | LCCN 2016004625 (ebook) | ISBN 978-0-399-55655-5 (trade) | ISBN 978-0-399-55656-2 (lib. bdg.) | ISBN 978-0-399-55657-9 (ebook)
Subjects: | CYAC: Building—Fiction. | Seasons—Fiction.
Classification: LCC PZ7.1.L59 (print) | LCC PZ7.1.L59 Fo 2017 (ebook) | DDC [E]—dc23

The illustrations in this book were created using watercolor and colored pencil, and finished digitally.

MANUFACTURED IN CHINA
October 2017
10 9 8 7 6 5 4 3 2 1

First Edition

Random House Children's Books supports the First Amendment and celebrates the right to read.

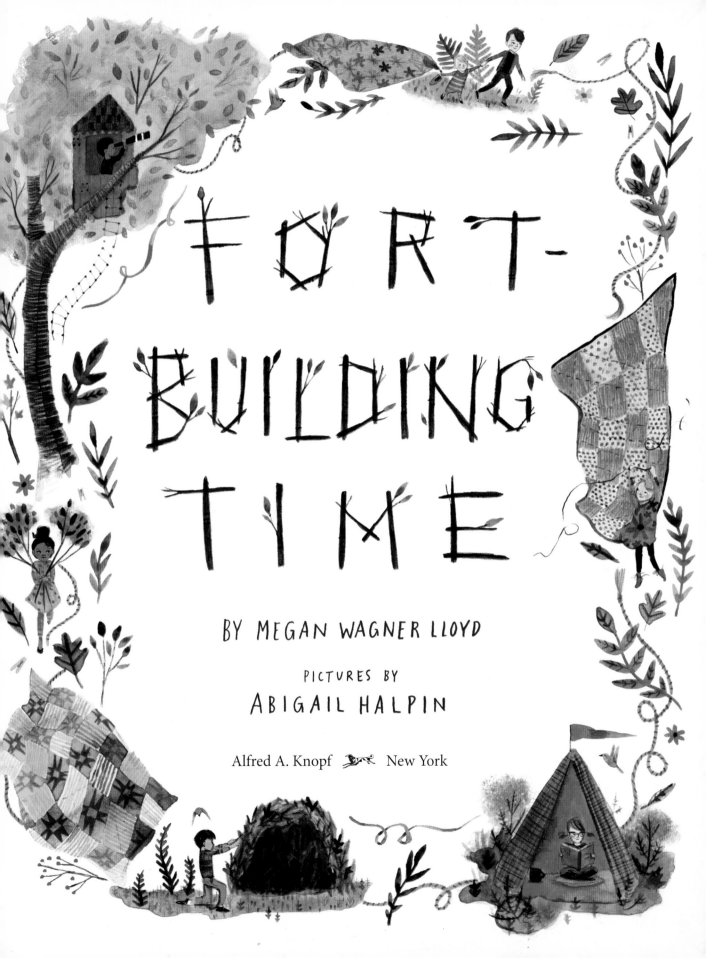

FORT-BUILDING TIME

BY MEGAN WAGNER LLOYD

PICTURES BY
ABIGAIL HALPIN

Alfred A. Knopf 🐾 New York

WINTER

is a snowball-throwing, scarf-wrapping, sled-pulling, ice-sliding time.

A dog-snuggling, cocoa-drinking, snowman-making, fort-building time!

SPRING

is a daffodil-hunting, umbrella-holding,
rain-watching, mud-squishing time.

A rainbow-finding, spaceship-drawing,
book-reading, fort-building time!

SUMMER

is a wave-racing, sun-sizzling,
saltwater-swimming, picnic-eating time.

A sandcastle-shaping, crab-digging, shell-stacking, fort-building time!

FALL is a leaf-chasing, wind-rocking, poem-writing, soup-sipping tim[e]

A sword-fighting, trail-climbing, woods-exploring, fort-building time!

Every season has its own secret-dreaming,
cozy-keeping, hush-listening, fort-building time.

So let's make today a
box-taping, clothespin-clipping—

OH NO!

Everything-slipping...
fort-FALLING time!

A project-fixing, secret entrance-crawling, spyglass-peering, fort-building time!